FOR JON

G. P. PUTNAM'S SONS
An imprint of Penguin Random House LLC, New York

Visit us online at penguinrandomhouse.com

Library of Congress Cataloging-in-Publication Data
Names: Thompson, Alexandra, 1987– author, illustrator.
Title: A family for Louie / written and illustrated by Alexandra Thompson.
Description: New York: G. P. Putnam's Sons, [2020] | Summary: A French bulldog
who loves gourmet food has trouble finding a family that is just right for him.
Identifiers: LCCN 2019033743 | ISBN 9781984813213 (hardcover) | ISBN 9781984813220 | ISBN 9781984813237
Subjects: CYAC: French bulldog—Fiction. | Dogs—Fiction. | Food—Fiction. | Families—Fiction. | Pet adoption—Fiction.
Classification: LCC PZ7.1.T4677 Fam 2020 | DDC [E]—dc23
LC record available at https://lccn.loc.gov/2019033743

Manufactured in China by RR Donnelley Asia Printing Solutions Ltd.
ISBN 9781984813213
1 3 5 7 9 10 8 6 4 2

Design by Semadar Megged and Nicole Rheingans
Text set in Granville
The art was done digitally.

A FAMILY FOR Louie

ALEXANDRA THOMPSON

putnam

G. P. PUTNAM'S SONS

Louie considered himself a
dog of very fine taste.

He knew every chef in town.

Each day, Louie explored the city. And along the way,
he stopped by his favorite restaurants for a meal . . .

like a tall stack of raspberry
pancakes with bacon
for breakfast,

spicy fish tacos with
salsa and guacamole
for lunch,

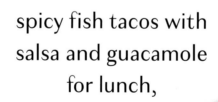

or a plate piled high with
fettuccine and meatballs
for dinner.

He always had room for dessert.

Louie ended each day
with a bath,

a good book, and
a hot cup of cocoa.
It was perfect.

Not one thing was missing from Louie's life.
He had everything he needed.

Well ... maybe there *was*
one thing missing.

It might be nice
to have a family,
thought Louie.

But he wasn't sure where to begin.

The next day, Louie saw
a family having a picnic
at the beach.

He thought he might ask to join them,
but when Louie approached…

they were eating green Jell-O salad
and sardine sandwiches!

Oh no! Louie's least favorite foods!
He couldn't possibly be a part of this family.

At his favorite sushi restaurant, Louie found
a family with an open seat at their table.

But when he tried
to sit down . . .

the seat wasn't
empty at all.

No, that wasn't the right
family for Louie either.

At the park, Louie met a family
having a barbecue.
Yum! Louie loved barbecue!

After lunch, the family invited
him to play Frisbee ...

but Louie just couldn't keep up.

It seemed like he would never
find the right family.

Feeling blue, Louie wandered down the street,
where he came across a brand-new bakery.
There he spotted a girl he had never seen before.

"Hi there!"
said the little girl.
"I'm Bea. Would you like
to try a cupcake?"

Suddenly, Louie felt a little shy.

But it wasn't long before
they became fast friends.

When Bea introduced him to her mother,
Louie tried to look as well-behaved and
handsome as possible.

"Can he come home with us? Please!"

Louie tried not to get his hopes up.

After what seemed like forever . . .

she agreed!

That night, Louie got a warm bubble bath …

and a home-cooked meal with his new family.

And it was perfect.